Just Grace,
Star on Stage

Just Grace, Star on Stage

Written and illustrated
by
Charise Mericle Harper

Houghton Mifflin Books for Children
HOUGHTON MIFFLIN HARCOURT
Boston   New York   2012

Houghton Mifflin Books for Children is an imprint of Houghton Mifflin Harcourt Publishing Company.

www.hmhbooks.com

The text of this book is set in Dante MT.
The illustrations are pen-and-ink drawings digitally colored in Photoshop.

Library of Congress Cataloging-in-Publication Data is on file.
ISBN: 978-0-547-63412-8

Manufactured in the United States of America
DOC 10 9 8 7 6 5 4 3 2 1
4500378530

For Linda Costelloe, who is a shining star!
I am happy to know you.

FIVE THINGS (GOOD AND BAD)

1. Being called Just Grace when your name is really just Grace. When there are three other Graces in your class at school, this is the kind of bad thing that can happen. I made a comic about it. (Bad Thing)

2. Having your best friend live right next door. (Good Thing)

ME   MIMI

3. Having an amazing grownup friend who is a flight attendant living in a fancy apartment in your basement. (Good Thing)
4. Having a dog named Mr. Scruffers. (Good Thing)
5. Having the teeny tiny superpower of empathy. (Mostly Good Thing)

When your Good Things list is longer than your Bad Things list, this means that you are lucky, and probably mostly happy.

MY LIFE IS GOOD.

WHY I WAS EXCITED ABOUT MISS LOIS ON A MONDAY MORNING

Monday mornings are not my favorite, and that's because Miss Lois, my teacher, always starts Mondays with spelling and math. It's hard to be excited about school when you are starting the day with the world's most boring subjects. Miss Lois says it's good to tackle the important stuff while our brains are fresh and rested from the weekend, but I know what the real truth is. Our brains might be rested, but more than that, they are in shock!

MY BRAIN

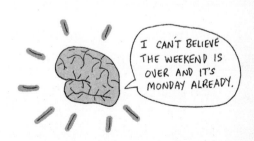

I CAN'T BELIEVE THE WEEKEND IS OVER AND IT'S MONDAY ALREADY.

When your brain is in shock, it's hard to make trouble.

OWEN 1 (CLASS TROUBLEMAKER)

The two people in our class who have perfect brains for Mondays are Sunni and Marta. They are super smart and always know the right answers. On Monday mornings, Miss Lois mostly lets the two of them answer all the questions. This is lucky for the rest of us, because it gives us extra time to get our brains awake. I wish this would happen for the rest of the week, but it doesn't. By Monday afternoon Miss Lois is back to her normal self, ignoring Sunni and Marta and picking on people who don't even have their hands up. I wonder how that feels? Being ignored on purpose. I bet they don't like it.

It probably makes them like Monday mornings more than any other time of the week.

My kind of brain is an imagination brain— it's not super excited about facts. That's why it was a surprise for me to be excited. But this wasn't a regular Monday. On this Monday Miss Lois said something she had never said before, and it changed everything. I never knew it, but one good sentence can do that— it can change everything.

WHAT HAPPENED NEXT

Everyone put their hands up and waved them around like crazy. Now we were all like Sunni and Marta. Nothing like this had ever happened on a Monday before.

Even though there were lots of people to pick from, Miss Lois did her usual thing and picked Sunni first. Usually when she does this no one cares, but today there was lots of groaning and complaining. Owen 1 even said, "No fair—she always gets picked." But Miss Lois didn't change her mind. She just looked at him and said, "Don't speak out of turn."

Normally Sunni's kind of a showoff when she talks in class, but today was different. When Miss Lois pointed to her, Sunni just sat looking nervous and stayed quiet. Finally Miss Lois had to walk over to her desk and ask her, "Sunni, do you have a question?" We all waited for what seemed like forever, and then finally she spoke.

7
· · · · ·

I was surprised about her question, and I wasn't the only one surprised because suddenly everyone was talking. Miss Lois waved her hand for us to be quiet, and said, "No one **has** to be in the play. If you don't want to act, you don't have to. There are going to be lots of ways to help with the play without being on stage. But don't think you can just watch and do nothing. This is a class project. Everyone has to participate." After she said that, there were even more questions than before. Sometimes answers are like that.

WHAT IS GOOD ABOUT MISS LOIS

Some of the people in our class don't pay attention. I know this because every time Miss

Lois talks about something new, the same thing always happens. Someone asks a question, and then two seconds later, right after she finishes answering it, someone else asks the *exact same question*. Miss Lois spends a lot of time saying the same stuff over and over again. It would drive me crazy, but I guess she's used to it.

Today the four most popular questions were . . .
1. Can I have one of the star parts?
2. Who chooses the parts?
3. Are we going to have to sing?
4. Do we get to wear costumes?

There were lots of other questions too. The funniest question was Valerie's:

IS IT GOING TO BE A LOVE STORY? BECAUSE I DON'T WANT TO KISS ANYONE!

I DON'T THINK THERE SHOULD BE KISSING.

The best part about talking about the play was that it took up almost all of our morning. We still had to do spelling, but everyone was so happy and excited that we hardly even noticed how boring it was.

MISS LOIS'S ANSWERS TO THE FOUR MOST POPULAR QUESTIONS

1. The star parts are going to be decided after everyone does an audition.
2. Ms. Perry is the director of the play, so she is going to choose the cast. We are very lucky to have her here for this special project. She is also a very good actress.
3. No, there will not be singing.
4. Yes, there will be costumes.

WHAT HAPPENED AT LUNCHTIME

Mimi and I talked about the play. There was a lot to talk about. We made a few guesses about what kind of play it could be, but really we had no idea. The only thing we were sure of was that it probably wasn't going to be a love story or a fighting story. Miss Lois said that the school had decided not to do those kind of plays. Both girls and boys were disappointed about that, but it was the same amount, so that was fair.

Even though Mimi and I are best friends, we sometimes like completely different things. I was excited about the *being in* the play, and Mimi was excited about the *helping with* the play. Her feelings about the play were a little more like Sunni's than mine, but

  that didn't mat-
ter—the amount
of excited we
were was the
same amount.

Just thinking about it made us both smile.

OUR PLAY DAYDREAMS

DAYDREAMING

Daydreaming is very different than night dreaming. Night dreaming is like riding on an amusement park ride that you know nothing about. Daydreaming is like riding on a ride that you made up yourself.

THE GOOD THINGS ABOUT DAYDREAMING

1. You can do it whenever you want.
2. It can be about whatever you want.
3. No one can stop you from doing it (even if they want to).

THE BAD THING ABOUT DAYDREAMING

Even though daydreaming is fun and good, there's one bad thing: the wanting-it-to-come-true part. Not all dreams can come true. Impossible dreams never come true.

POSSIBLE DREAMS	IMPOSSIBLE DREAMS
BE A STAR ON THE STAGE.	WIN A TRIP TO THE MOON.
BECOME A FAMOUS SINGER.	KISS A FROG AND TURN IT INTO A PRINCE.
FIND $1,000 ON THE STREET.	FLY JUST BY MOVING YOUR ARMS.
SEE A DOUBLE RAINBOW	FIND A POT OF GOLD AT THE END OF A RAINBOW.

WHEN HOPING YOUR DREAM WILL COME TRUE IS A GOOD IDEA

When you are the only one having the dream.

WHEN HOPING YOUR DREAM WILL COME TRUE IS A BAD IDEA

When lots of other people have the exact same dream as you.

THE DREAM OF BEING A STAR ON STAGE

My dream was not a good idea—I was 100 percent sure of this. Even though no one else was talking about it, there was no way that I was the only one in my class having the star on stage dream. Probably ten or maybe even eleven other people were having the same dream too.

SOME THINGS THAT ARE TRUE ABOUT PLAYS

1. Plays have starring parts.
2. Not every part is a starring part.

3. Not everyone gets to have a starring part.

Knowing this made me know some other things.

THE OTHER THINGS

1. Not all of us who wanted starring parts were going to get starring parts.
2. The ones who didn't get starring parts were going to be disappointed and sad, and maybe even crying.

I WONDER WHO IS HAVING THE SAME DREAM AS ME?

SNEAKY EYES ARE LOOKING AROUND

Mimi was lucky. Her dream was not a super popular one. She had a better chance of it coming true than I did. That's probably why she could smile without having sneaky eyes.

WHAT WOULD HAVE BEEN A GOOD THING TO DO

Pick a different dream.

WHAT IS IMPOSSIBLE TO DO

Pick a different dream.

Once a dream is stuck in your head it's hard to change it, even if you know that keeping your dream could make you sad, jealous, unhappy, angry, and a whole bunch of other not-good feelings.

It's worth it.

WHAT HAPPENED AFTER LUNCH

PATTERN OF THE FIRST
TWENTY MINUTES

At first Miss Lois was good about answering questions, but after a while I could tell that she was getting mad. She was trying to teach us about triangles and angles, but all anyone wanted to do was talk about the play.

Miss Lois has two faces: her normal face and her upset face. And now her normal face was slowly changing into her mad face. No one noticed it happening except me. Even though I didn't mean to, I said, "Uh-oh" out loud. Miss Lois didn't hear me, but Owen 1 did. He sits right behind me. "What's wrong?" he said. "Did you burp?" Owen 1 is not a nice,

quiet boy. He is a loud, annoying boy! That's
why I did not feel one
bit sorry for him when
Miss Lois told him to
go to the quiet desk in
the hall.

HOW RULES ARE MADE

When Miss Lois gets mad she doesn't scream
or yell. What she does is worse. She makes up
new rules! Rules are worse because screaming and yelling only lasts for a few minutes.
Rules can last forever!

OUR NEW RULES

1. No talking about the play unless Miss
   Lois says we can talk about the play.
2. No questions about the play unless

Miss Lois says we can ask questions about the play.

Five minutes later, after she had given us the new number one rule and the new number two rule, Miss Lois had to give us a new number three rule. The new number three rule was all Brian Aber's fault.

3. No pretending to be in the play while still in class.

Mostly this was a rule for Brian Aber, Robert Walters, and Owen 1, because nobody else

PROBABLY THINKING HI-YAH!

PRETENDING HIS PENCIL IS A SWORD.

in class was going to swing their pencil around and pretend it was a sword.

Brian Aber didn't care about Miss Lois's

new rule. I could tell this because instead of drawing triangles like the rest of us, he was staring straight ahead at nothing.

Rule number 3 was going to be a hard one for Miss Lois to make happen. If someone is behaving perfectly good on the outside, there's nothing you can do about what they are doing on their insides.

Even though we weren't supposed to, Brian Aber and I probably weren't the only ones daydreaming.

That's probably why nobody got much done for the whole rest of the day.

WHAT MISS LOIS DID THAT WAS GOOD

Finally Miss Lois noticed, because for the last thirty minutes she gave up trying to teach us stuff and said we could talk about the play instead. It was only for a little bit, but still, it was better than doing work. Everyone had different ideas about the play. After each question Miss Lois just mostly shook her head no. It was almost impossible to find any yes answers.

SOME OF THE QUESTIONS OUR CLASS ASKED

- Can we do fighting on the stage?
- Is there a part for a princess riding a unicorn?

- If we do fighting, can we use ketchup for fake blood?
- Is there going to be dancing?
- Is there going to be a slide to play on?
- Is there one of those spotlight things? Can it shine on just me?
- Can my dog be in the show? She knows a really cool trick, but we have to give her a hot dog.
- Are there pirates in the show?
- Can we have glow-in-the-dark costumes and turn out all the lights?
- Do we get to wear makeup?
- Do we have to wear makeup?
- Is it mostly a girl kind of show?
- How many people can fit on the stage? Will it break if everyone jumps up and down at the same time?
- Is there going to be an intermission thing and snacks?

- Do we get flowers at the end of the show?

My favorite question was the flower one. I liked that idea—for sure I was going to tell Mom bout that. I even had a little daydream about it.

WHAT MISS LOIS NEEDED TO DO

I had a feeling that some kids had never seen a play before. At least that would explain why Sarah and Isabella were thinking there were going to be swings and slides on stage. For sure Miss Lois needed to help them with that, and maybe even explain what a play was.

WHAT HAPPENED ON THE WAY HOME

Both Max and Sammy said they wanted to be in the play. This was a surprise. Some people you can imagine being on the stage, and some people you can't. Sammy was a "can't." He has trouble remembering regular school stuff, so I didn't know how he was going to remember a whole bunch of words that in his own brain hadn't thought up. It seemed pretty impossible, but I didn't say anything because I didn't want to be the person to break his dream bubble.

SAMMY'S DREAM BUBBLE

The only part of acting that I was sure Sammy would be good at is the not-getting-embarrassed-in-front-of-an-audience part. For that he was perfect. Sammy doesn't care one bit what other people think.

WHAT IS HARD TO DO

It's hard to wait for something to happen when you are excited about the something that is going to happen but don't know very much about it. This sounds confusing and it is—both for your brain and your feelings.

I'M EXCITED!

I CAN'T WAIT.

I DON'T KNOW EXACTLY WHAT I'M WAITING FOR.

When I got home I wanted to tell Mom about the play, but that was impossible to do right away. Mr. Scruffers always wants all my attention the minute I walk in the door. She barks like crazy and acts like she hasn't seen me in months. It's usually around 450 minutes, but for her I guess it seems longer. Dad says dogs don't have the same sense of time as humans do. It takes me 450 minutes to walk to school, spend the whole boring day there, and then walk home. It sounds more impressive if you change the time to seconds. When I told Mom the seconds number even she was impressed.

27,000 SECONDS IS SUCH A LONG TIME.

MR. SCRUFFERS BEING SAD

Mr. Scruffers's most favorite thing to do is to chase squirrels, but by now the squirrels know this, so they don't really come into our yard anymore. I think she misses them. Now she only gets to see them when we go on a walk. When we are at home she mostly just has to be happy chasing Crinkles every now and then.

WHAT MOM TOLD ME ABOUT ACTING THAT WAS A SURPRISE

When I told Mom about the play she was really excited and surprised, and then she had a surprise for me too. She said that before Augustine Dupre became a flight attendant she used to be an actress. She said some more things too, but I sort of stopped listening because my brain was still thinking, *Wow! An actress!*

Usually when Mom knows that I am thinking about going downstairs to visit Augustine Dupre she starts saying things like

1. "Why don't you wait until you see her outside?"
2. "Maybe you should call first."

3. "I'm sure she is busy—you can see her tomorrow."

The whole reason for this is that Mom is worried that Augustine Dupre will think I am a pest, but this is impossible because friends aren't pests and Augustine Dupre and I are friends. I've told Mom this about a thousand times, but she still doesn't believe me—at least she didn't until today. Today she surprised me, because instead of saying the usual, she said, "Why don't you go and see if Augustine Dupre has any acting tips for you?" I know Mom, so before she could change her mind and go back to normal, I turned around and ran straight downstairs to Augustine Dupre's apartment.

WHAT I ALWAYS DO

Every time I visit Augustine Dupre, I do a special knock on the door so she knows it's me. I started doing this because of Crinkles. When I was at the door, Crinkles could stay in Augustine Dupre's apartment, but if Dad was at the door, Augustine Dupre had to grab Crinkles and put him outside super fast. That's because Dad had a No Pets in the House rule, but after we got Mr. Scruffers, he pretty much had to change that.

At Augustine Dupre's wedding, Dad found out about Crinkles and how Augustine Dupre had been sneaking him into her apartment. It was a surprise for him, but he surprised us back, by not being one bit upset about it.

CRINKLES HAS LOTS OF LOVE FOR AUGUSTINE DUPRE

I CAN GET PAST THAT DOG. I'LL DO IT FOR AUGUSTINE DUPRE.

WHAT I HAD TO GET USED TO

Now that Augustine Dupre is married, it's not always her that answers the door. Sometimes it's her husband, Luke. At first this was kind of weird, but now I'm kind of used to it—plus in the daytime, it's still mostly Augustine Dupre. Luke is a UPS deliveryman, so he works in the day.

After I knocked, Augustine Dupre answered right away. Sometimes I get lucky and she's in the middle of making something yummy like croissants or cookies, but today she wasn't. As soon as she opened the door

MOM SAYS YOU WERE AN ACTRESS. CAN YOU HELP ME GET A STAR PART?

AUGUSTINE DUPRE

I told her all about the play and how I needed her help. Mom says it's nicer to do a little chit-chatting before you ask for something, but I was too excited for chitchat. I couldn't help it.

Augustine Dupre was surprised. It took her a minute to get her brain used to my question. She put her hand on her head and said, "Well, that was a long time ago. Let me think."

I watched her while she was doing her thinking and tried to imagine her on stage. Sometimes when you get new information about a person it can change the way they look to you. I had never noticed it before, but Augustine Dupre really does have an actress look. For a half-second I even felt a tiny bit shy, but then it was gone and I was back to normal.

MY VISIT WITH AUGUSTINE DUPRE

Augustine Dupre and I like to do most of our talking while sitting at her kitchen table. Usually she offers me lemonade or something, but today we didn't have anything. I guess she was too busy thinking about acting to think about snacks.

At first I was kind of disappointed with her advice, because she was saying things like *You have to be yourself; Don't be afraid; If you feel good about yourself others will too.* This is the sort of stuff Mom says, and she's not even an actress. I didn't want this kind of advice. What I needed were real acting tips, the kind of things to help me get a starring part.

ME AS A STAR

Augustine Dupre likes talking, but she really loves talking about acting. I didn't know this. She talked for a long time, and then at last, after what seemed like forever, she finally said something good.

AUGUSTINE DUPRE'S ADVICE

Be loud and clear; Do not whisper. If you are on stage people in the back of the audience will want to hear you. Practice projecting.

THE IMPORTANT FUN THING I LEARNED

Augustine Dupre gave me a lesson in projecting. Projecting is not what it sounds like—it has nothing to do with pictures.

PROJECTOR

PUTTING A PICTURE ON THE WALL

PROJECTING

TALKING LOUD AND CLEAR SO THE PEOPLE ALL THE WAY BACK IN THE AUDIENCE CAN HEAR YOU.

The most important thing about projecting is that you have to do it without shouting. It's not as easy as it sounds. Augustine Dupre said I would for sure get better at it if I practiced. I was hoping she was right.

I told her I was going to be the best projector around, and then we both laughed, because that sounded funny. The only one who did not think projecting was fun was Crinkles. As soon as we started making our voices louder he jumped off the sofa and ran to hide.

I ADMIT IT! I'M A SCAREDY-CAT.

CRINKLES UNDER THE SOFA.

WHAT I DID AFTER I LEFT AUGUSTINE DUPRE'S APARTMENT

When I came back upstairs I told Mom about projecting, and then I gave her a demonstration. Mr. Scruffers was not like Crinkles. As soon as I did the loud talking she got excited and started barking. This gave Mom the idea to send me outside to take Mr. Scruffers for a walk before dinner. This was not what I wanted to do. I wanted to practice acting stuff instead.

THE LUCKY THING

Just as I was putting on my shoes the doorbell rang. It was Mimi and her little brother, Robert. Before I could say anything Mimi said, "Can Robert run around in your backyard with Mr. Scruffers? He needs to burn off some energy. He's driving us all crazy." I looked down at Robert. He nodded. Mom must have been listening, because she shouted at me from the other room.

YOU CAN GO TO THE BACKYARD NOW, BUT AFTER DINNER WE ARE GOING TO TAKE THAT DOG FOR A WALK!

I grabbed Mimi's arm and pulled her to the back door before Mom could change her mind. As soon as I opened it, both Robert and Mr. Scruffers took off running. I'm not sure how Mr. Scruffers feels about being chased by Robert, but I'm sure how Robert feels about it. He loves it!

HOW TO BE A GOOD FRIEND

Even though Mimi does not want to be in the play she practiced projecting with me. The backyard was perfect for it, because there was lots of space and we could move back and test out if we could still hear each other.

Mimi was really good at it—better than I was. It was lucky that she was not wanting to be on stage, because if we were competing, for sure she would get it. Mimi said she was probably good at <u>projecting</u> because of all the shouting and yelling she did at Robert. She was right about that—Robert listens more if your voice is loud and yelling. That's probably how an <u>audience</u> worked too.

We stayed outside until Mom called me in for dinner. I was glad about that because my throat was hurting. People might think acting is easy, but it's not—even just the talking part is hard work.

THE THING THAT HAPPENS AT BEDTIME

Every night before I go to bed I do the same three things.

1. Put on my pajamas.

2. Brush my teeth.

3. Flash my bedroom lights on and off for Mimi.

Mimi and I are super lucky. Our bedroom windows are right across from each other. Usually stuff like that only happens on TV.

MIMI'S WINDOW

MIMI'S WINDOW

WHAT I SEE BEFORE SHE FLASHES HER LIGHT ON.

WHAT I SEE WHEN SHE FLASHES HER LIGHT ON.

Once I was in bed I closed my eyes and tried to concentrate on imagining myself as an actress. I don't know how you're supposed to control a night dream, but imagining yourself as the thing you want to be right before you fall asleep seems like it could work.

The first thing I thought of when I woke up in the morning was *I didn't dream anything!*

WHAT HAPPENED AFTER THAT

I got disappointed, and then I got grumpy. It was the first time ever that I was mad about a dream that didn't happen—a not dream.

Sometimes after a bad dream you can be sad, but this was different. It was the nothing that was making me sad.

WHAT MADE THINGS WORSE

As soon as I walked into the kitchen Dad said, "What's wrong with you? Did you get up on the wrong side of the bed?" Saying stuff like that to a grumpy person is a bad idea. It does only one thing, and that one thing is make the grumpy person even grumpier!

WHAT MADE THINGS BETTER

I made a face at Dad to show him I was mad at him, but it was wasted because he was eating his oatmeal and didn't even look up.

As soon as Mom saw me, she knew something was wrong. She came over and put her hand on my shoulder. "Did you have a bad dream?" she asked. For a half-second I thought about lying and saying yes. Mom is always super nice to me if I've had a bad dream. But it's hard to lie so early in the morning, so instead I just told her the truth.

I was surprised. I thought she would tell me I was being silly, but instead she gave me hug and said, "It's hard to be disappointed." She was right. It is.

WHAT MIMI SAID ON THE WAY TO SCHOOL

When I told Mimi about my not-happening dream, she said something that made me feel a whole lot better.

By the time we got to school, both of us could hardly wait for class to start. This was unusual. If Miss Lois had known it she would have been excited.

WHAT TREVOR SAID WHEN EVERYONE GOT INTO CLASS

"Can we talk about the play instead of doing work?" Usually Trevor says stuff that no one else agrees with, but today he said exactly what everyone else was hoping for, too. When Miss Lois nodded yes and smiled, we all knew that Trevor had asked the exact perfect question at the exact perfect time. Trevor put his arms up and said, "YES!" He was probably thinking, *Finally, I've done something right.*

WHAT WAS HARD TO REMEMBER

Everything Miss Lois told us about the play. She said a lot of stuff. After she finished explaining everything she gave us some handouts to take home.

Miss Lois told us to put them away, but not everyone listened to her. Sammy snuck a peek—I saw him. Suddenly he was waving his paper in the air and shouting. "The show is going to happen in only two weeks! It says so right here. Look, it's on page three!" Instantly Miss Lois stopped smiling. She hates it when people don't listen to instructions—plus Sammy had done two other things wrong too.

WHY SAMMY WAS IN TROUBLE
FOR SURE

MISTAKE **1**: LOOKING AT THE HANDOUT.

MISTAKE **2**: NOT PUTTING HIS HAND UP.

MISTAKE **3**: SHOUTING IN CLASS.

That was three mistakes all at the same time. I could tell what was going to happen next, and it was not going to be good.

WHAT MISS LOIS DID THAT SURPRISED ME

Instead of getting mad Miss Lois said, "We'll talk about the play for ten more minutes, just to clear up some details, but then that's it." Of course everyone had questions, but Miss Lois said, "No questions. I'm the only one who is going to do the talking, and I'm going to tell you why I'm excited about the play."

THE THING MISS LOIS WAS EXCITED ABOUT

Miss Lois said her favorite thing about the play was that it was going to be a great learning tool. Right away that probably made everyone feel a little less excited. I don't know how she could have missed Owen 1 making a loud groaning sound, but she did.

She said, "The play is equal parts fun and learning." When a teacher says this, you can't always believe them about the fun part. Grownups have different feelings about fun than kids do.

WHAT	FUN FOR KIDS	FUN FOR ADULTS
SHOPPING	NO	YES
EATING IN A RESTAURANT	SOMETIMES	YES
JUST STANDING TALKING	NO	YES
LEARNING NEW FACTS	SOMETIMES	YES

WHAT HAPPENED AT LUNCH

Even though we were supposed to keep our play handouts in our backpacks, we didn't. Everyone wanted to know as much about the play as possible. It was a good thing to do, because there were a few things on there I didn't know about.

THE NINE THINGS I LEARNED ABOUT THE PLAY FROM MISS LOIS

1. The play is about the life cycle of plants.
2. It is not going to be just a long list of boring facts. (She promised!)
3. There is no singing or dancing.
4. The main girl part is the forest fairy queen.
5. The main boy part is the king.
6. The other main part is the narrator, which sounds kind of boring.

7. The other characters in the play are forest fairies, king's knights, and talking trees and animals.

8. There are lots of ways to help with the play without being in it. You can make costumes, make the sets for the play, make the program for the play, and lots of other stuff.

9. The play director is Ms. Perry and she is very nice and very fair and she is also a real actress.

THE TWO THINGS I LEARNED ABOUT THE PLAY FROM THE HANDOUT

1. If you want a starring part you have to go to an audition.

2. The show is going to be at night in the auditorium, and we get to invite guests.

The last page was all about the auditions. I'm glad I already knew what that was. Some of the other people didn't.

Everyone who wanted to have a main part or be a king's knight or forest fairy had to go to the audition. There was a form for parents to sign and it must have been super important because in big red letters it said, MUST

BE RETURNED TOMORROW. If you wanted to be a talking plant or a talking animal you didn't have to audition—I guess anyone could do those parts.

Right away I could tell that getting the queen fairy part was not going to be easy. There are girls who play pretend fairies every day at lunchtime. For sure some of them were thinking that they would be perfect for the fairy queen part. I looked around the playground to see if I could see them, and there they were: Olivia, Marta, Grace W., and some girls from another class, all dancing around like perfect little fairies. They were good. Mimi saw me looking at them and said, "You'd be a much better fairy." It was a nice thing for her to say, but they were experts at moving their arms around gracefully and skipping around on their tiptoes. Just because your name is Grace does not mean you are graceful.

THE ONE THING I ABSOLUTELY DO NOT WANT TO HAPPEN

THIS IS THE WORST PART EVER!

I HAVE BEEN A TREE IN A PLAY BEFORE. IT IS NOT A GOOD PART TO HAVE.

WHAT I DID WHEN I GOT HOME

I took Mr. Scruffers straight outside so I could practice doing fairy moves in the backyard.

WHAT MR. SCRUFFERS DID NOT LIKE

Mr. Scruffers had never seen me do fairy

arms before. It took a lot of "No!s" before she finally stopped jumping up and trying to grab my sleeves.

Mom must have been watching me from inside, because after a few minutes she came out to see what I was doing. It wasn't one bit funny when she said, "Are you trying to be an octopus?" After I got upset, she said she had only been joking, but part of me didn't know if I should believe her or not. Octopus arms were definitely not something I wanted to do at my audition.

After Mom went back inside I tried to move my arms differently so I wouldn't look so much like a sea creature, but it was hard to get the octopus picture out of my brain.

BE LIKE ME!

I WANT TO GRAB YOUR WAVY ARM.

WHAT AUGUSTINE DUPRE TOLD ME

Augustine Dupre must have seen me too, because all of a sudden she was outside as well. It's hard to do fairy arms in front of an audience. I stopped moving and suddenly felt kind of embarrassed. "What are you doing?" she asked. I told her about the fairy queen part, and how I had to do an audition to get it. I was hoping that she knew some fancy fairy secrets, but she said no, she didn't know anything about being a fairy. "If they want you to act like a fairy, they will teach you to act like a fairy," said Augustine Dupre. "I think you will have more luck if you keep practicing the projecting." And then she said the thing that made me feel a whole lot better. "I don't think good fairy arms is going to get anyone the part of the fairy."

WHY THIS WAS GREAT NEWS

1. Because my fairy arms looked more like octopus arms.
2. Because Marta will not get the starring part the minute she walks into the room.
3. Because my arms were kind of tired.

As she was walking away I asked Augustine Dupre one more thing. "Can you come to the show?" She turned around. "Grace, I'd love to!" she said. "Thank you." Augustine Dupre had never come to my school before. Just imagining her being in the audience and watching me on stage was exciting. I think it was a good luck sign.

WHO DOES NOT LOVE THE THEATER

Mom and Dad! They have no appreciation

for the fine art of acting. After only about five minutes they made me stop practicing my projecting at the table.

Mom said it was annoying, and Dad said his ears were starting to hurt.

I told them that it was going to be their fault if I didn't get the part in the play, but they didn't care. Mom said, "Go practice in your room." But I had a better idea.

In the shower, I was the queen of projecting.

WHAT WAS UNUSUAL

I woke up super early. For some reason, I couldn't wait to get to school. Nothing exciting was going to happen, but still I wanted to get there—it must have been play energy.

I CAN'T STOP THINKING ABOUT THE PLAY.

On most days Mimi comes to my house to get me, but today I was ready early, so I went to get her. It took her a while to get to the door. She said that Robert was being annoying and hiding all her stuff. As soon as Robert heard me he came running up to see me. "Hi, Grace!" he shouted. I was just saying hi back when all of a sudden Mimi grabbed him. "Where's my other sock?" She gave him a serious look and pointed to her feet. She was wearing one blue sock and had one bare foot. Mimi made a pretend angry face, but Robert wasn't scared. "The sock monster took it!" he shouted. Then he squirmed away and ran off laughing. Mimi rolled her eyes and said, "I'll never find it. Let me put on different socks. I'll be right back." While I was waiting I decided to practice my fairy arms, just in case. That's probably why I didn't notice Robert sneaking back into the room. And that's definitely why I didn't notice him getting ready to throw Mimi's rolled-up sock. But I did notice being hit on the side of the head. Something like that is hard to miss.

THINGS THAT MAKE A DIFFERENCE

Nobody likes to get socked. Most often it will make you mad, but sometimes the mad part depends on other things too.

GETTING SOCKED

WILL MAKE YOU MAD	WILL NOT MAKE YOU MAD
- PERSON WHO THREW SOCK IS LAUGHING AT YOU IN A MEAN WAY. - THE SOCK IS A DIRTY, SMELLY SOCK. - THE SOCK HIT YOU IN THE EYE AND HURT YOU. - THE PERSON WHO THREW THE SOCK IS NOT SORRY.	- PERSON WHO THREW SOCK IS LAUGHING BUT HE IS CUTE. - THE SOCK IS A CLEAN SOCK. - THE SOCK DID NOT HURT YOU. - THE PERSON WHO THREW THE SOCK IS TOO LITTLE TO BE SORRY.

I looked at Robert, and even though I was a little bit mad, I had to smile. He was so happy with himself—plus he was giggling like crazy. I threw the sock back, but he missed catching it. He was a better thrower than a catcher. By the time Mimi came back downstairs we were throwing it back and forth from the hallway all the way to the kitchen. "Well, that's helpful," said Mimi. "Don't encourage him." "Too late," I said. "He's encouraged. Plus he's a good thrower." "Yay! I'm a good thrower," shouted Robert. Then he said it over and over again, nonstop. I couldn't tell if he was being annoying on purpose or by accident, but it was nice not to have to stick around to find out. "Time to go!" said Mimi, and we walked outside and closed the door.

"Sometimes I like going to school, just to get a break," said Mimi. I nodded my head. I could see what she was meaning.

MIMI'S SOCK.

SCHOOL

It's not a good thing when the most exciting part of your school day happens in the first ten minutes of school. That's what happened today. After everyone sat down Miss Lois collected the permission forms for the auditions, and then that was it. The whole rest of the day was pretty much regular and boring. Even Owen 1 didn't do anything interesting. He got himself sent to the hallway, but it was just for playing with the Velcro on his shoes and making too much noise. It was nothing unusual.

WHAT WAS NOT GOOD

I could see how many people wanted to audition for the big parts in the play. Miss Lois had a lot of forms in her hand. And mostly they were from girls! A lot of the boys wanted to be talking plants or animals. I wasn't surprised that Sammy didn't want to be a talking animal. Sammy is pretty much scared of anything that has four legs and fur.

STAY AWAY FROM ME, FURRY BUNNY!

BUNNY IS SUPER CUTE

WHAT CAN MAKE YOU WORRIED AT LUNCHTIME

Mimi and I ate lunch outside with Grace F. and Grace W. From where we were sitting I could see Marta and her gang of fairy girls. They were all prancing around doing their fancy fairy moves, and not one of them looked like an octopus. Grace W. saw me watching them and said, "Marta only wants one thing for her birthday, and that's to be the fairy queen in the play." "Her birthday? What do you mean?" I asked. "Her birthday is on the day of the play," said Grace W. "So it would be perfect if she got the fairy queen part. It would be her dream come true!" Grace W. put her hands together and closed her eyes like she was wishing it for Marta.

"I want to be a forest fairy," said Grace W. "What do you want to be?" I couldn't talk. My brain was too busy thinking of every-thing I had just heard.

Finally Mimi came to my rescue. "Grace wants to be the fairy queen. It's too bad that there can't be more than one fairy queen." Grace W. looked surprised. "Well, I wouldn't want to be sad on my birthday," she said. It was confusing. What did she mean? Mimi is good at telling when something could be an argument, so she changed the subject really fast and asked Grace F. what she wanted to do for the play. I was glad to hear that she was like Mimi. She didn't want to be on the stage.

Listening to Grace F. gave me and Grace W. a break from talking about Marta, which was good on the outside, but on the inside I still couldn't stop thinking about it.

It was easy to say, "I hope you get the part

you want" to Grace W., but it would have been impossible to say that to Marta. I was glad she wasn't sitting with us. In fact, it was im-

possible for my brain to even think about saying it to her. I couldn't help it. I just had to add the word "don't."

SOME HARD THINGS

Sometimes Sammy and Max walk home with us, but today it was just Mimi and me. I was glad about that. I needed to ask Mimi some questions, and I didn't want Sammy and Max listening in.

QUESTION ONE

Do you think people will think that Marta should get the fairy queen part because the play is on her birthday?

The first thing Mimi said was "That's a hard question." Then she stopped walking and thought for a while. Finally she said, "It's too bad that Marta's birthday is on the play night, because if she doesn't get the part she is for sure going to be sad—and no one should be sad on their birthday. But it's not really fair for Marta to get the fairy queen part only because it's her birthday." Then she made a big sigh and said, "That was a hard question!" She was right—it was.

QUESTION TWO
Should I feel guilty about wishing that Marta doesn't get the part?

Mimi swung her arms up and said, "Stop asking me all these hard questions!" Then she looked at me with her sad Mimi eyes. Instantly I had no choice—I had to do what she wanted. I changed the subject. Sad eyes have that kind of power, but only if you are careful about using them. If you use them all the time, they lose their power. Mimi hardly ever uses hers, so they're super strong.

MIMI USING HER SAD EYES

"Okay. Okay," I said. "I'm sorry." On the outside I listened to Mimi talk about her costume ideas, but on the inside my brain was being just like Robert's brain. It was thinking the same thing over and over again. Only my brain wasn't thinking, *I'm a good thrower. I'm a good thrower. I'm a good thrower.* Mine was thinking: *Please, Marta, don't get the part. Please, Marta, don't get the part. Please, Marta, don't get the part.*

It probably wasn't a good thing to do, but I just couldn't stop myself.

WHAT MIMI AND I DID WHEN WE GOT HOME

We took Mr. Scruffers and Mimi's brother, Robert, for a walk around the block. It's surprising, but Robert is a lot more work than Mr. Scruffers. He's kind of like one of those super bouncy balls—you never know where he is going to go next. Now I could see why Mimi was so good at projecting.

After the walk Mimi and Robert came over. Robert went to the backyard with Mr. Scruffers, and Mimi and I stayed in the kitchen. Even though I hadn't been talking about it, I think Mimi could tell that I was still thinking about the play and Marta. Mostly that was because I kept talking about the audition and asking her what she thought I was going to have to do. Mimi is like me: she's never been to an audition before. Sometimes talking about stuff helps you feel better, even if no one comes up with any answers.

Mimi could tell that I was suffering. I think that's why she said what she said. She was trying to make me feel better, only it didn't work that way. It worked the opposite way!

WHAT MIMI SAID TO ME

"You shouldn't worry so much about Marta.

There are other people in our class who are going to be trying for the part too."

WHY THIS WAS NOT HELPFUL

Now there were even more people to worry about, and up until this second I had totally forgotten about them.

Mimi looked over and smiled. She was hoping that I was feeling better. Sometimes it is hard to do the right thing, even if you know you should. Sometimes the wrong thing comes out of your mouth, and even though you have the power to stop it, you don't. This was one of those times.

WHAT I SAID TO MIMI

"I bet there are lots of kids in our class who like to sew just like you do. I bet a bunch of them are going to want to do costumes too." Mimi looked surprised. This was not what she was expecting. I don't think she had thought of this before either. Now she was worried just like I was. For a second I thought, *Ha! Now you know what it feels like.*

But that only lasted for a few seconds, because the next thing I thought was *I shouldn't*

have said that. Suddenly my empathy power was working. It was not a good feeling.

SAD + GUILTY

WHAT I SHOULD HAVE SAID NEXT

"I'm sorry, Mimi. That was a mean thing to say."

WHAT I SAID NEXT

Nothing.

After a few more seconds of quiet, except for Robert yelling and screaming in the background, Mimi said she had to go. Robert made a big fuss about having to leave, but Mimi didn't let him win. She pretty much dragged him out the door.

Sometimes when you are sad, you just want to be alone.

DINNER MAGIC

For the whole of dinner, Mom and Dad tried to cheer me up. They are good at it. By dessert I was feeling a whole lot better, and even told Mom the thing about giving flowers to someone at the end of a play. She said she already knew about that, and then she winked at Dad. That's her not-so-secret way of telling him, "Let's remember to do this." I smiled. Getting flowers would be good.

Being in a better mood made me happy, but it also made me feel guilty about Mimi. It was not fair for me to be happy and for her to still be sad.

After dinner I just had to call her. It's hard to tell if someone is happy or sad just by hearing a "hello" on the phone. Mimi's sounded normal, but I couldn't be sure.

WHAT IS NOT EASY TO DO

It's not easy to apologize, even on the phone.

THE GOOD THING ABOUT A BEST FRIEND

They always forgive you.

BEFORE BED

Mimi and I flashed our lights at each other. This time it felt extra special. I did mine six times, one for each letter of BFFIMI, which means *best friends forever I mean it!* And I really did! I meant it a lot!

THE THING THAT SHOULD NOT HAVE HAPPENED

I slept in. I couldn't believe it. I never sleep in, ever! I don't know how it happened. The last thing I remembered was closing my eyes, and then suddenly Mom was yelling at me to get up. It was a disaster. I had no time to try on a special audition outfit, practice my projecting, practice doing fairy arms, or do anything at all! I hardly even had time to eat breakfast.

The whole thing was very strange. Even Mr. Scruffers had slept in.

WHAT YOU CAN'T DO AT SCHOOL

Even though I had free time, I did not practice my projecting or my fairy arms at lunchtime. These were not things I wanted to do when other people could see me doing them. Was that a bad sign?

If you have never been on stage, it's hard to know if you have stage fright. I didn't think I had it, because in my imagination I imagined myself being on stage, and it did not scare me one little bit. But I did have field fright—I could not imagine myself standing out there all by myself doing fairy arms.

STAGE VERSUS FIELD

If you do strange things on stage, people know you are acting. If you do the exact same things in a field, people will think you are weird. It was that simple. One was good and one was bad.

BAD

GOOD

IN A FIELD

ON A STAGE

WHAT WAS GOOD

The best part of the whole day was the fifteen minutes right before school ended. Miss Lois was in such a good mood that she let us all talk about the play. She probably knew that people were nervous about the auditions. She said that tomorrow was going to be a big day too. It was the day when everyone who was not in the play was going to get to sign up for the jobs they wanted. Mimi was probably going to be as nervous tomorrow as I was today. We weren't going to be calm until our names were right there on the lists, where we wanted them to be.

FAIRY QUEEN
GRACE STEWART

COSTUME DESIGN
MIMI BURNSIDE

THE AUDITION

After school Mimi walked with me to the auditorium. I was thinking she could maybe stay and watch, but a sign on the door said that only those people doing auditions could come in. I was kind of sad and kind of glad about that. Sad because I wanted Mimi in there with me, but glad because I didn't want a bunch of other kids just sitting there watching and making fun of everyone.

Mimi gave me a good-luck hug and I went in. I've been in the auditorium a hundred times, but today it felt different. Normally when there are a bunch of kids in there, everyone is talking and pushing and joking around, but today it was different: everyone was quiet. I sat down next to Grace W. and said hi. Marta was sitting on her other side. I didn't say hi to her.

WAITING AT THE AUDITION

All of a sudden someone sat next to me. It was Max. "Have you seen Sammy?" he asked. I shook my head no. "I sure hope he gets here in time. He had to go and get his form. Do you think Miss Lois is right about no singing? Because I'm not doing this if I have to sing." Max looked at me and waited for an answer. He was talking a lot more than normal. I couldn't tell for sure, but he was probably nervous too. "Miss Lois is usually right about stuff," I said. "If she says there's no singing, I bet there's no sing-ing." Max nodded. I couldn't tell if he felt better or not, but him being worried made sense. Max was not an excellent singer.

I was hoping that Max would keep quiet, but he didn't—he kept talking. "What part do you want?" he asked. He said it really loud. Now everyone around us was going to listen to what I said next. Even though the answer was fairy queen, I couldn't say fairy queen. Not with Marta sitting almost right next to me, and it being her biggest birthday wish. If I said fairy queen everyone would hate me. So I lied. It was a little lie, but it was a helping lie and not a hurting lie, so I think it was okay.

Max nodded his head like he understood, but he didn't, because the next thing he said was, "What's a narrator?" Sometimes even if you know what a word means it's not always easy to explain it to someone else, but I tried anyway. I looked around to see if anyone else was listening, but couldn't tell. "It's a person who tells a story, or tells stuff about the story as it's happening," I said. "Is it a fun part?" asked Max. I made a list in my brain of all the things I knew about the play.

THE PLAY

1. It's a play about the life cycle of plants. LEARNING STUFF

2. Miss Lois said it teaches us stuff. BOR-ING

3. It has a king, some knights, and some fairies in it. FUN PARTS

4. It has talking trees and animals in it. SILLY PARTS

5. It has a narrator. BORING PART THAT

TELLS ABOUT THE LEARNING STUFF

EVEN THE NAME "NARRATOR" SOUNDS KIND OF SERIOUS.

AND A LITTLE BIT BORING.

I looked at Max and said, "You're right—it's probably not so much a fun part, but it's an important part. The narrator does lots of explaining about what's happening in the story." "Oh," said Max. "Well, I want to be a knight, but I hope you get it." I made sure my fingers were double crossed behind my back and then I said, "Yeah, me too!" But I didn't mean it! Not one little bit.

I was glad when Ms. Perry came on stage to talk to us. Talking to Max was making me nervous.

WHAT MS. PERRY WAS LIKE

Ms. Perry was exactly like what I thought a play director-actress person would be like. She had crazy hair and cool glasses and could talk really loud. She was also wearing different clothes than a normal person would.

JUMPSUIT

Ms. Perry did some talking about the play, and then she asked for volunteers. I was surprised that not every hand went up. If Ms. Perry wanted a helper, I was going to be her number one helper.

HOW TO GET SOMEONE TO PICK YOU

This is a normal hand up.

This is the "PLEASE PICK ME" hand up.

This is the "PICK ME OR I WILL DIE" hand up.

Ms. Perry looked right at me. I was 100 percent sure she was going to pick me, but then right before she did, she looked away. Instead of me, she pointed to someone in the back of the room. "You! You, walking down the aisle. Can you come up here?" asked Ms. Perry.

When you don't get picked and you really want to be picked, you always have to look right away to see who was picked instead of you. When I saw who it was, I couldn't believe it. It was Sammy! He waved his permission slip in the air and said, "I forgot this so my mom had to bring it." "That's fine," said Ms. Perry. "Now just come up here and stand beside me. Don't worry—it's nothing bad." Then she looked around the room and said, "Now I need two more volunteers." This time everyone put their hands up. I guess they were thinking, *If Sammy can do it, then I can do it too.* I was waving like crazy, but now with a bunch of other people waving, Ms. Perry was never going to see me.

ME WISHING I HAD A GIANT HAND

SHE WOULD SEE ME NOW.

WHO GOT PICKED

Ms. Perry picked Ruth and Owen 2. Even though I was sad that Ms. Perry didn't pick me, I was a little bit glad that she didn't pick Marta either. I would not have been happy about that.

WHAT HAPPENED ON STAGE

Ms. Perry pointed to the three people on stage and said, "Okay, now I want you all to dance." It was not what anyone was expecting—none of them moved. She said it two more times so they would know she really meant it, but still no one danced. I think it would have been easier if there was music, but there was nothing. It's not easy to dance to quiet. Finally Ms. Perry went over and danced next to them, to give them dancing energy. Sammy did a few extra things with his hands, but Ruth and Owen 2 pretty much just moved their feet back and forth.

All of a sudden Ms. Perry rang a little bell and told them to stop. I could tell they were glad about that. She asked them each to pick two words to describe how they felt while they were dancing. I was not surprised that all three of them used *embarrassed* as one of their words. Suddenly I was feeling pretty happy that I wasn't up there on stage. I would have been embarrassed too!

I thought they were going to come back and sit down, but instead, Ms. Perry gave them each a hat and a scarf and told them to put them on. Of course Sammy couldn't be normal. He wrapped the scarf around his legs so it looked like a giant diaper, and didn't even wear the hat. I bet Ms. Perry noticed that— Sammy is not the best with directions. When they were all dressed up Ms. Perry rang the bell and said, "Dance!" This time it was completely different. Everyone moved around a lot more than before.

Sammy was the best. He was dancing crazy, like a giant, weird baby.

SCARF

It was so funny! I don't know if we were supposed to be quiet, but it was impossible. Everyone was laughing. I looked over, and even Ms. Perry was smiling. Of all the kids, Sammy was the star.

THE POWER OF THE STAGE

Ms. Perry rang the bell again and said, "Stop." Everyone stopped, and this time when she asked the same question as before, no one used the word *embarrassed*.

Even after everyone came back and sat down, Sammy was still a star. People were smiling at him and giving him the thumbs-up sign. Sammy didn't say anything, but I could tell he was kind of surprised. Normally he doesn't get this kind of attention for acting crazy, but that's because he's usually standing on the ground. Being up on the stage makes everything different.

WHAT HAPPENED NEXT

Ms. Perry asked us to think about why the people on stage had been embarrassed the first dancing time and not the second dancing time.

WHAT THE PEOPLE ON STAGE SAID
Wearing the costumes was fun so they
felt like dancing more.
They got over the scared part the first time.
They were used to the stage by the
second time.

I was glad when she picked me to talk. I said,

"With the costumes on they felt like they were not really just themselves—they were kind of like characters in a play." Ms. Perry smiled after I said my answer. I felt good about that.

IF YOU CAN DANCE ON STAGE FOR TWO MINUTES AND HAVE FUN, THEN YOU WILL BE FINE IN THE PLAY.

THE AUDITION, PART ONE

Everyone got split into groups of four. My group had Max, Grace W., and Marta in it. Mostly that was because we were sitting in the same row. I couldn't decide if that was a good thing or a bad thing, that me and Marta were going to be on stage at the same time.

When it was our turn to go up, we picked out a hat and a scarf, and then when Ms. Perry rang the bell, we started dancing.

WHAT WAS EASY AND FUN

Dancing on stage.

I didn't wear the scarf in a weird way like Sammy had. A lot of the boys were trying to be funny like Sammy, but mostly the girls were like I was, more normal.

WHAT WAS NOT SO EASY

To see what Marta was doing from where I was dancing. Max was next to me and I couldn't see anything on the other side of him. He was like a wild monkey. His arms and legs were everywhere, even upside down. Not everyone can do a handstand while dancing. I'm sure Ms. Perry was impressed. Even though I couldn't see her, I was pretty sure that Marta was dancing around like a fairy. The best I could do was an octopus trying to be a fairy.

WHAT IS BETTER THAN AN UNDERSEA CREATURE

When our turn was over we went back and sat down. I couldn't tell if I had done a good job or a bad job. Max had definitely done a god job! I told him that I liked his upside-down dancing. He smiled and said, "Your Egyptian dancing was good too." It wasn't the compliment I was hoping for, but Egyptian dancing was a lot better than octopus dancing. I smiled back and said, "Thank you."

GAMES

When everyone had gotten a chance to dance, Ms. Perry put us into two groups to play some games.

ANIMAL BALL

You stand in a circle and throw the ball to someone. If you get the ball you have to pretend to be an animal until someone guesses what your animal is. If they guess right, then they get to throw the ball next.

FREEZE TAG TELL ABOUT YOURSELF

Like regular freeze tag, but if you are tagged you have to tell two things about yourself.

When it was my turn to talk I made sure

that I did a super good job of projecting. Most of the other kids were pretty quiet and hard to hear, but not me. Even if Ms. Perry had been standing way at the back of the auditorium she would have for sure heard me. I said a little in-my-head thank-you to Augustine Dupre. Her acting tip was being really helpful.

MY NAME IS GRACE STEWART AND I HAVE BEEN IN A PLAY BEFORE!

HOW I WAS HELPFUL

When Ms. Perry said she needed a volunteer to help give out pencils and paper I was the first one with my hand up. We had to write down three things on our paper.

1. Our names.
2. The part we were hoping to get in the play.
3. Why we wanted that part.

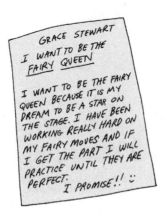

THE ONE THING I REALLY WANTED TO SEE

Marta's paper.

I know that she wrote down *fairy queen*, but what I really, really, really wanted to see was what she put down for *why*.

WHAT WAS A SURPRISE

I really thought there would be more audition stuff to do, but Ms. Perry said it was over and we could all go home. I couldn't believe we were done. It was kind of disappointing that it didn't last longer.

Ms. Perry said the names of all the parts, and who got what, would be on the board outside the front office in the morning. I was wondering if she had already done her deciding, but I couldn't tell by looking at her. She told everyone the same thing, "Good job," and then pointed to the door.

WHAT I WAS GLAD ABOUT

I walked home with Sammy and Max. They were excited about the play and talking a lot. That helped; it made me feel less worried. Sammy said he was disappointed that there wasn't a giant baby in the show, because if there was, he knew he would for sure get the part! He was right—he would. Max said that dancing on stage had been fun, but still he didn't want to do it in front of a bunch of other people, especially parents! Doing it in front of grownups and strangers would be different, but I'd still do it. I wasn't nervous like he was. A real actress can't be scared of anything.

SURPRISE AT HOME

When I got home Mr. Scruffers did not jump on me the minute I walked in the door. It felt weird. For a second I thought something bad had happened, but then I heard barking in the backyard.

SURPRISE IN THE BACKYARD

I looked outside and saw Mimi and Robert running around with Mr. Scruffers. As soon as Mimi saw me she came running over. "How was it? What happened? Was it fun? Did you get the part?" She had a ton of questions. Just as I was about to answer, I got clonked in the head by a ball. It was Robert, playing catch again. I was lucky he had picked the big red ball and not the little green ball.

GREEN BALL	RED BALL
HARD RUBBER	SOFT AND FILLED WITH AIR
DIRTY AND COVERED WITH DOG SLOBBER	KIND OF CLEAN
STINKY	NO SMELL

"ROBERT!" yelled Mimi. "Say you're sorry." "Sorry," said Robert. He looked like he was about to cry. "I'm okay," I said. "But next time tell me before you throw." Robert nodded, but he still looked sad. "Like this," I said. I got the ball and shouted out to him. "Robert, catch!" And then when he looked up, I threw it to him. He's terrible at catching, so of course he missed, but he didn't seem to mind—he ran after it and he was smiling. I tapped my hands together so he would know to throw it back. It was a perfect throw. He really was a good thrower.

WHAT IS HARD

It's not easy to tell a story and play catch at the same time. Especially if there is a dog who really wants you to play with the green ball instead of the red ball.

* MEANS   THROW THE BALL FOR ME!
I CAN'T BELIEVE YOU AREN'T
THROWING THE BALL FOR ME.
COME ON! THROW THE BALL
FOR ME!

We stayed outside longer than I wanted, because after I finished playing catch with Robert I had to throw the ball for Mr. Scruffers. I would have done it earlier, but it took Robert a long time to get tired. It was weird, but Robert wouldn't let Mimi play catch with him—he only wanted to do it with me. I tried to get Mimi to throw the ball for Mr. Scruffers, but she said it was too disgusting to touch. Not everyone can deal with dog slobber.

WHAT MIMI AND I DID BEFORE BED

Tonight Mimi and I flashed our lights seventeen times. That's a lot more than normal, but it was worth it. We did one flash for every letter of GOOD LUCK TOMORROW! — and even one for the exclamation point. I was really hoping it was going to help.

NIGHT DREAMING: TRY NUMBER TWO

I closed my eyes and tried to imagine myself on stage. It didn't seem like it would be that hard, since all I had to do was think back to the afternoon, but for some reason every

time I tried to imagine myself on stage, someone else
was there too. Sammy! And
not normal Sammy. Sammy
in a scarf diaper! This was
not something I wanted to
dream about.

WHAT WAS GOOD ABOUT THE NEXT MORNING

As soon as I woke up and thought about my
night, I was happy.

Sometimes a nothing can make you happy.

When Dad saw me he noticed my joy because he said, "What are you so happy about?" I laughed because even though it was impossible to explain, I couldn't wait to answer him. "Nothing," I said, and it was 100 percent the truth.

WHAT MIMI ASKED ME ON THE WAY TO SCHOOL

At first she didn't ask the exact question she wanted to ask. Instead she said, "If you don't want to, you don't have to, but I have to ask you something." Of course I was confused. "What?" I asked. "What is it? Tell me." "It's nothing exciting," said Mimi. "It's just a favor." Now I was super curious. "WHAT? What is it?" When Mimi asked the question, it was not what I was expecting.

"Why?" I asked. "Because Robert is driving us all crazy by asking for you. He asks about it every ten minutes, and he won't play catch with anyone else. Not me, not Mom, and not even Dad. It's only you! It's okay if you don't want to do it, but I promised him I would ask you."

MY ANSWER

When I said yes Mimi clapped her hands together and said, "Thank goodness! I was hoping you'd say that, because I already told Robert yes." It was hard to be annoyed about that, because Mimi was so happy. PLUS she agreed to run all the rest of the way to school. We couldn't wait to get to the board. I wanted to see my name next to *Fairy Queen,* and Mimi wanted to write her name in the costume helper section.

WHAT WE SAW IN THE PLAYGROUND

Usually I don't see Marta in the mornings, but today she was by the slide with her fairy friends. They were all hopping and skipping around like perfect little fairies. "I wonder why she's not looking at the board?" I said. "Maybe she forgot?" said Mimi. "Or maybe the paper isn't up yet." I thought about that for a second. It seemed like a good answer. Maybe she had gotten here too early. "Maybe it's up now," I said. "Let's go see." Mimi turned and we ran to the front of the school. Normally Mimi and I do not hold hands at school, but this was a special occasion. I needed extra friend energy. Right before we went in I grabbed her hand.

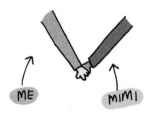

THE FIRST THING WE SAW IN THE SCHOOL

Lots and lots of kids all crowded around the board. It was not going to be easy to get in there and find my name. "They must have just put this up," I said. All of a sudden Max was standing in front of us. He was smiling. "I got the knight part and you'll never guess who is going to be the king." He didn't even give us a moment to guess, because two seconds later he yelled, "IT'S SAMMY!" I couldn't believe it. "No way!" I said. "Yes way!" said Max. "It's true! You can go see for yourself." He pointed to the board. "It says so right on the paper." I let go of Mimi's hand and pushed forward to see. "Plus you're going to be super happy when you see your name," said Max. "You got what you wanted!" Now I really pushed ahead.

Mostly it's not nice to push, but I couldn't help it. I had to get closer and see. "Stop pushing!" said a voice in front of me. It was Sunni. She was mad. "And you're not the fairy queen! Marta is!" "What?" It was all I could say. I was confused. Why was she being so mean? Why was she lying? Maybe she felt bad for Marta. I tried to ignore her, but she kept talking.

Then slowly everything made sense.

WHAT IS KIND OF IMPOSSIBLE TO DO

Keep from crying, even if you really don't want to cry.

WHAT HAPPENED NEXT

Mimi grabbed my hand and pulled me to the bathroom.

THE FIRST THING I ASKED MIMI WHEN I COULD TALK AGAIN

"Did you see it? Is it true?" Mimi nodded yes. Suddenly I was crying even harder than before. The bell rang for class, but I didn't care. I cried and cried and then I stopped, just like that, but the weird thing was I still heard crying. Then suddenly I knew it wasn't just me. The bathroom was full of crying girls! I looked at Mimi, and without me even asking she said, "Three others." It was so sad. We all wanted to be the fairy queen, and now here we were sitting in the bathroom crying. It was terrible.

THE THING THAT I HEARD THAT WAS A SURPRISE

I could have said, "You can have my part— I only wanted to be the fairy queen," but I didn't. I didn't say anything. I still wanted to be in the play, and the narrator was for sure better than a talking tree. I washed my face to get rid of the crying marks, and then Mimi and I walked to class. "Are you going to be okay?" asked Mimi. I tried to say yes but no sound came out. After you have been crying a lot your voice doesn't always work right. Plus sometimes talking makes you start crying all over again.

HOW MISS LOIS SURPRISED US

Even though we were late, Miss Lois didn't ask any questions or even get mad. She just said, "Girls, please take your seats." I put my head down so no one could see my face. The last thing I wanted was for everyone to know I'd been crying. I especially did not look at Marta. I'm sure she was smiling. When you look at the ground you notice different things than normal. Marta was wearing ballet slipper kind of shoes. That explained a lot.

IT'S EASIER TO WALK LIKE A FAIRY WITH THESE ON.

THE REST OF THE MORNING

I was kind of surprised that the morning went by fast. Maybe it was because we started late, or maybe it was because I wasn't looking forward to lunchtime. I couldn't tell which.

LUNCHTIME

After we ate lunch, Mimi and I went back to the message board at the front of the school. With all my unhappiness Mimi never got a chance to put her name down on the costume maker list.

It was the first time I was going to see my name next to *Narrator*. Part of me hoped it wouldn't be there. That maybe Ms. Perry had made a mistake, but fixed it, so now my name was going to be where it should be, right next to *Fairy Queen*. I was hoping this, but I knew it wouldn't be true. While Mimi wrote her name down, I got brave enough to look, and there it was, just like everyone said.

NARRATOR - GRACE STEWART

It wasn't disappointing. It wasn't exciting. It was just there.

The biggest surprise was seeing Sammy's name next to *King*. I knew it was going to be there, but still when I saw it, I had to say, "I can't believe it," out loud.

WHAT WAS A SURPRISE

That Ms. Perry was standing right behind me

when I said, "I can't believe it." She didn't know I was talking about Sammy. She thought I was talking about me, and the part I was getting. I know this because she said, "You were the best one for the part! Congratulations."

I know I shouldn't have, but I had to ask her about the fairy queen part. "Why didn't I get to be the fairy queen?" Ms. Perry didn't seem surprised, but what she said was a big surprise to me. A huge surprise! And not a good one!

OH. I THOUGHT ABOUT YOU FOR THE FAIRY QUEEN, BOT YOU HAVE SUCH A CLEAR, LOUD VOICE THAT IS EVEN MORE PERFECT FOR THE PART OF THE NARRATOR.

I couldn't talk. All I could do was make my

I-can't-believe-it face. Mimi knows that face, so she saved me. She said hi to Ms. Perry, and then kept her busy talking. "I really want to work on the costumes," said Mimi. Ms. Perry said, "Super! We are going to need a lot of help, so I'm glad you are excited to chip in." Ms. Perry smiled at me again, and then turned to leave. As she was walking away she said, "Don't forget, meetings start Monday after school for the helpers, and today after school for the actors."

THE FIRST THING I SAID TO MIMI

"Did you hear that? I would have gotten the part of the fairy queen if I hadn't done that stupid projecting thing! Augustine Dupre was wrong! She gave me the wrong advice. It ruined everything!"

AUGUSTINE DUPRE RUINED EVERYTHING!

← HANDS IN ANGRY FISTS

WHAT I DID NEXT

I stomped off to the playground.

Mimi followed me, but she had to run a little bit to keep up, because stomping is faster than regular walking.

WHY THIS WAS A BAD IDEA

The first person I saw was Marta. She was with Sunni. Seeing them together was not a good thing. It was terrible.

AFTER LUNCH

Sometimes drawing comics makes me feel better. I'm not supposed to draw in class, but

Miss Lois wasn't looking at me so I did it anyway. When I was done I didn't feel any better.

WHAT HAPPENS MOST OF THE TIME

Usually when I'm mad I start to feel better after some time has gone by, but today was different. I just felt the same, right up until the bell rang to go home. Only I didn't get to go home. I had to go to the play practice and watch Marta do the part that I would have gotten if I hadn't listened to Augustine Dupre.

WHY I AM AN EVEN BETTER ACTRESS THAN EVERYONE KNOWS

I went to the play practice and did an excellent job of pretending that nothing was wrong.

WHAT I LOOK LIKE ON THE OUTSIDE

WHAT I FEEL LIKE ON THE INSIDE

WHAT WE DID

Ms. Perry gave us all copies of the play, and we read through the first ten pages together. My narrator person had a lot to say.

THE TWO THINGS I WAS RIGHT ABOUT

1. The narrator had to say a lot of facts.
2. It was not a very fun part.

My part reminded me a lot of Miss Lois. Just standing in front of people by yourself and doing lots of talking. It wasn't exciting and excellent.

I WANT TO TELL YOU SOME INTERESTING THINGS ABOUT TRIANGLES.

I WANT TO TELL YOU AN INTERESTING STORY ABOUT PLANTS AND A KING.

MISS LOIS, THE TEACHER

ME, THE NARRATOR

MY LAST CHANCE

I'm Marta's understudy. An understudy is a person who learns all the lines for a part but only gets to go on stage and do the part in an emergency. I have to study all of Marta's lines and know them by heart. If Marta gets sick or something happens and she can't do the play, I'll get to be the fairy queen. Not a lot of people want to be an understudy, because it's mostly a lot of work for nothing. Ms. Perry was pretty surprised when I volunteered. She said it was unusual for actors to have two big parts to learn, but I gave her my sad eyes and she finally nodded her head and said okay. She kind of had to—I was the only person who volunteered.

Only two people have an understudy. Marta has me, and Sammy has Owen 2. I thought I would have one too, but Ms. Perry says if I get sick she's going to do my part. That's probably because she knows she's never going to be able to get anyone else to want to learn all my boring lines.

WALKING HOME

I walked home with Max and Sammy. Max was the only happy one out of the three of us. I was grumpy and Sammy was worried.

DO YOU THINK MS. PERRY WOULD GIVE MY PART TO OWEN 2 IF HE GOT BETTER AT THE PART THAN ME?

After Sammy finished talking I had my own little daydream.

Would Ms. Perry give me Marta's part if I was super good at it? I told Sammy not to worry but secretly wondered if Marta was worried about me too.

BEING HOME

As soon as I got home I took Mr. Scruffers out to play in the backyard, and then it happened: the most terrible thing that has ever happened in the whole history of my backyard.

THE TERRIBLE THING

The terrible thing started when I saw Augustine Dupre watching me from her window.

Seeing her brought back all my mad feelings. I was so mad, I ignored her when she waved at me. Augustine Dupre knows me, so she could tell something was wrong. Two minutes after me not waving, she came outside to find out what it was. "What's wrong, Grace? Are you okay?" she asked. I tried to hold it in, but I couldn't—it came out. The truth is not a bad thing to say, but what can make it a bad thing is the way you say it.

After I finished talking I started to cry. Augustine Dupre put her hands up to her mouth. She was super shocked.

Sometimes when you don't know what to say and are feeling really uncomfortable, the only thing your body wants to do is escape. That's probably why as soon as Augustine Dupre said, "Oh, Grace! I'm so sorry!" I dropped Mr. Scruffers's ball and ran into the house and up to my room. Poor Mr. Scruffers—I didn't even let her follow me. I left her out in the yard with Augustine Dupre.

WHAT HAPPENED NEXT

Mom heard me. She followed me upstairs but then had to go back down again because someone was knocking at the back door. I knew it was Augustine Dupre. Ten seconds later Mr. Scruffers jumped on my bed. It took a lot longer for Mom to come back upstairs, and when she did, she was not happy.

WHAT MOM WAS MAD ABOUT

HOW COULD YOU TALK TO AUGUSTINE DUPRE LIKE THAT?

Even after I told Mom about the narrator part, and how I would have for sure gotten the fairy queen part except for Augustine Dupre's advice, she was still not any less mad. She said, "You asked Augustine Dupre for her advice, but it was your choice to follow it. Plus, I find it hard to believe that you're so sure you would have gotten that other part." This was not what I was expecting. Mom patted my shoulder, but I could tell that she was not feeling super sorry for me. "Isn't the narrator a main part?" she asked. I nodded yes, but said, "It's not a good one, though." Mom shook her head. "Well, I don't know what to say. At the very least you need to apologize to Augustine Dupre."

WHAT HAPPENED AFTER MOM LEFT

I did lots of thinking. Mostly it was thinking of how I had made Augustine Dupre sad. I'm not sure Mom was 100 percent right about not blaming Augustine Dupre, but she was kind of right about the apology part. I had been mean.

WHY IS THIS PLAY MAKING ME SO MEAN?

My empathy power was getting tired of me making the same mistake over and over again.

HOW TO MAKE THE BEST APOLOGY LETTER EVER

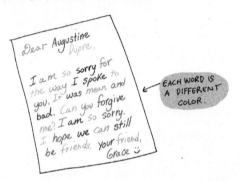

Dear Augustine Dupre,

I am so sorry for the way I spoke to you. It was mean and bad. Can you forgive me? I am so sorry. I hope we can still be friends. your friend,
Grace ☺

← EACH WORD IS A DIFFERENT COLOR.

WHAT I WAS GLAD ABOUT

Mom didn't ask to see the letter. Usually she's kind of nosy about stuff like that, but this time she said, "Don't show me. This is between you and Augustine Dupre." She didn't even stop me when I said I wanted to give it to her right away, even though it was dinnertime and all the food was on the table.

WHAT WAS DIFFERENT

For the first time ever I felt kind of uncomfortable doing my special knock on Augustine Dupre's door. I was worried she was mad and would ignore me. But I was wrong. After a few seconds she was there, holding the door open. I couldn't look at her face—it was too hard to do. I stuck out my hand and offered her the note I had made. It took a lot longer for her to read it than I thought it would. Maybe it was all the colors—the yellow parts were kind of hard to see. Finally, after what seemed like forever, she said, "Oh, Grace, I am so sorry it didn't work out for you, and thank you for this lovely letter."

WHAT WE DID NEXT

We had a little hug and I cried some more. Augustine Dupre invited me in, but I said I couldn't. It was dinnertime. As I was walking up the stairs she said, "Am I still invited to the show?" After everything I had said to her, I couldn't believe that she still wanted to come. I looked at her face and nodded. I was lucky. Augustine Dupre is just like Mimi—good at forgiving.

WHAT HAPPENED THAT NIGHT

Mimi and I flashed our lights six times like usual, and then I went to bed. Two seconds after I put my head on the pillow, I fell asleep. It was record fast. I didn't even have time to think about what I wanted to be dreaming.

THE FOUR MAIN THINGS I DID SATURDAY AND SUNDAY

1. Play catch with Robert.
2. Draw comics.

3. Play with Mr. Scruffers.

4. Go back and forth between my house and Mimi's house.

WHAT IS INTERESTING

I had never tried before, but you can really play catch with a lot of different things. Some work better than others. By the end of Sunday, Robert and I were kind of experts at it.

THINGS YOU CAN PLAY CATCH WITH

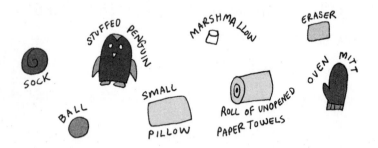

SOCK

STUFFED PENGUIN

MARSHMALLOW

ERASER

BALL

SMALL PILLOW

ROLL OF UNOPENED PAPER TOWELS

OVEN MITT

WHAT I DID NOT DO

Practice my projecting.

MONDAY MORNING

Mimi was at my door fifteen minutes early. I was glad that she came over to get me. I was getting a little tired of all the catch playing, and I'm sure if I had gone to get her, Robert would have thrown something at me.

Normally Mimi and I walk to school, but today she wanted to run. She could hardly wait to see if her name was on the costume list. I didn't feel like running, but I didn't complain. It was my turn to be a good friend for her. When we got to school hardly anyone was on the playground—we were that early. I thought the school might not even be open yet, but we were lucky: it was. This time there wasn't even one other person at the board. Mimi found her name really easy, and it was just where she wanted it to be.

COSTUME DEPARTMENT
MIMI BURNSIDE

WHAT WAS DIFFERENT ON MONDAY MORNING

Ms. Perry must have had a talk with Miss Lois, because after we finished our math work Miss Lois said we were going to skip spelling and read the play instead. Miss Lois handed everyone a copy of the play. It was the first time that people who were not in the play were seeing it. Everyone was excited. Right away I could tell that this was going to be way more fun than spelling.

READING THE PLAY

Miss Lois read all the parts. I thought she was going to let us actors read our own parts, but she said it would be faster if she did it. I think she was wrong about that. She's not a super-fast reader, plus she kept stopping every couple of minutes to talk about stuff. There were a lot of true facts in the play, and every time Miss Lois read one, she stopped reading so we could talk about it.

A lot of the true facts were narrator parts. I could tell my part was really important, but it was also kind of scary. There was lots of stuff to memorize. Now I was thinking that remembering our regular spelling words would have probably been easier.

THE STORY OF THE PLAY

The play is about a king who lives next to a forest. He has a bunch of knights with him and he likes to make them do silly things because he gets bored a lot.

One day the king decides that he wants his knights to tear down the forest that is next to the castle. He wants to have a view of the mountains that are on the other side of the forest.

He takes his knights to the forest to start chopping down the trees, and that is where he meets the fairy queen, queen of the forest fairies. She tells him he can't chop down the forest. The king says yes he can, and he doesn't care about the forest because it's just a bunch of plants. Then the lesson part of the play starts. The fairy queen shows the king all the animals that live in the forest and how they work together with the plants to keep the forest healthy. There are some funny parts in there. It is not as boring as I thought it would be.

In the end, the king decides not to chop down the forest, and instead makes the knights build him a higher bedroom so he can look over the forest and see the mountains.

THE FUNNY PARTS

I was glad about the funny parts. It made the learning parts more fun. The king part was the most funny. I could see why Ms. Perry had picked Sammy. If Sammy could dance on stage like a giant baby, he could for sure do all the king stuff.

THE THREE MOST FUN THINGS SAMMY GETS TO DO

1. Throw a pretend seed into the audience and have someone throw it back at him. It's for the part where the king says he can do what the animals do. Birds take seeds far away and drop them to help new plants grow in new places. The king says he can do this too, so he tries to throw a seed really far, but the wind just throws it back at him. For this part the person in the audience is kind of like the pretend wind. When Sammy throws the seed at them they are supposed to throw the seed back to Sammy. Sammy asked, "How is this going to work?" but

Miss Lois said, "Don't worry,—Ms. Perry knows what she's doing."

2. Act silly and faint when a talking bear tells him that he helps plants by eating berries and then pooping the seeds out in different places. This one is perfect for Sammy. He loves anything to do with poop.

3. Use a pretend slingshot and shoot a seed at a bell to make it ring. This happens at the very end of the play. The forest fairies like bells, and it's the king's way of saying thank you to them for making him save the forest. All the boys in class were crazy jealous about the slingshot part.

Miss Lois made up a new rule right away. She was smart—it was probably an important one.

WHAT WAS A SURPRISE

The fairy queen part is not so different from my part. She has to say a lot of learning stuff too, but she doesn't do her talking all by herself. She gets to talk to the other fairies and the king. Plus, even though I don't know what her costume is, I bet it's better than the narrator costume.

THE BIG ANNOUNCEMENT

Miss Lois said we are going to study plants in class and make displays about what we learn, so that on the night of the show our parents can come into the classroom and see what we have been doing. I thought that was going to be it, but she had more to say. She said that every afternoon from now until the play we are going to work on play stuff instead of regular school stuff. Nobody was sad about that.

Instead of coming back to the classroom after lunch, everyone will go to their special room to work on the play. My special room is the auditorium. Mimi's special room is the lunchroom. It's too bad we can't be together.

LUNCHTIME

Mimi was kind of disappointed that the lunchroom looked the same as normal. She was hoping it would have all sorts of costume stuff in it, but it didn't. For the whole lunch-time she wanted to stay where we could see the lunchroom door, just in case anything exciting was going to happen. Finally when lunch was almost over we saw two school workers and lady go in there with a bunch of boxes. "That's probably the costume lady," said Mimi. "She looks nice, doesn't she?" I nodded. It made Mimi happy. I was glad when the bell rang. It's not much fun to stand around looking at a door.

THE LUNCHROOM DOOR

THE PRACTICE

I've decided something new. I like my part! Ms. Perry said I should show emotion and project as much as I can. At first I didn't understand what she was talking about, but then she showed me how to do it. It's not at all like being Miss Lois. I was wrong about that. It's much better!

I WANT TO TELL **YOU** AN IN·TER·EST·ING STORY ABOUT **PIANTS** AND A **KING**.

↑
I USED LOTS OF STYLE WHEN I SAID IT THIS TIME.

I was hoping to find out what my costume looked like, but Ms. Perry said it was too soon for that. She did tell me two things about it though:

1. I get to hold a stick and point to stuff.
2. I get to hold a book that has all my lines in it, and some of them I don't even have to memorize. I can just read them.

THE
KING'S
TALE

THE BOOK THAT I
GET TO LOOK IN TO
SEE MY LINES.

This was a big relief. I smiled super big
when Ms. Perry gave me the book. She noticed because she said, "That's how I like my
actors—happy."

THE OTHER GOOD THING ABOUT MY PART

I get to stand at the side of the stage and
watch everyone do their parts. Ms. Perry said,
"It's a lot of standing around for you," so she
gave me my own special chair. Nobody else
gets a chair—it's so cool. From watching everyone practice I can tell that Marta is better
at her part than Sammy is at his. This was not
a surprise to me, but for some reason it was a
surprise to Marta.

Ms. Perry told Sammy not to feel bad, because it was still just the first day and lots of people were doing stuff wrong.

WHAT IS NOT THE BEST THING

The people who are helpers with the play get to go home at the normal time, but the people who are actors have to stay an extra hour. This means that I don't get to walk home with Mimi for almost two whole weeks!

Today, after practice I walked home with Sammy. Max had already gone home, because people with small parts were allowed to leave at the regular time too.

What Sammy said surprised me, but it was a good idea. It was a good way for me to learn Marta's part. I didn't tell Sammy this, but when the play first started I had a secret wish.

I was glad that my secret wish was slowly being less true. It's not comfortable having a wish that hopes that something bad happens.

Sammy and I practiced his part and Marta's part all the way home. He was definitely getting better. I don't know if I should have told him this, but I did. I think it made him happy. Plus it was true.

YOU HAVE THE BEST PART IN THE WHOLE PLAY.

WHAT HAPPENED WHEN I GOT HOME

After taking Mr. Scruffers for a walk, I went over to Mimi's house. Robert tried to surprise me by throwing a stuffed penguin at my head, but I was ready for him. Robert was getting better at catching, and I was getting better at having a conversation while playing catch. It was a win for both of us.

WHAT I WAS NOT HAPPY TO FIND OUT

I'M SORRY, GRACE. YOUR COSTUME IS NOT GOING TO BE VERY FANCY.

IT'S NOT BAD, BUT IT'S JUST NORMAL-LOOKING.

THE COSTUME

BLACK SHIRT

WHITE COAT

LITTLE HAT

GLASSES

BLACK PANTS

What Mimi said was not good news, but for some reason it didn't make me cry. Maybe I was getting used to being disappointed about the play, I couldn't tell, but I was glad I didn't burst into tears.

A GREAT THING ABOUT THE PLAY

Miss Lois is not giving us any homework until the play is over. It was so nice to have lots of free time; I studied my play lines and then drew a comic. Even though practicing the lines for my part was kind of like studying, it was different and better than schoolwork.

WHAT HAPPENED AT NIGHT

Mimi and I have a new flash sign. It's seven flashes—each flash is for one letter of YAY PLAY. We are going to do it right up until the night of the play.

WHAT I DIDN'T KNOW

Sometimes when you are working really hard the time goes by faster than normal.

NORMAL DAY

BUSY DAY

This is how the whole rest of the week was. Only two unusual things happened all week.

UNUSUAL THING NUMBER ONE

On Wednesday, Marta was back to being grumpy, even though Sammy was doing a really good job with his king part. She was so grumpy that Ms. Perry finally had to have a private talk with her. Of course everyone wanted to know what was going on, but Ms. Perry took her to the little room at the back of the auditorium. It's impossible to hear what's being said in there if the door is closed, and she closed the door. After about three minutes Ms. Perry stuck her head out and called my name. Everyone looked at me like I was going to get into trouble. Even though I didn't do anything wrong, I kind of felt like maybe they were right. Walking to that little room felt like walking to the principal's office. I was nervous.

Ms. Perry is not a person who wastes time. As soon as I was in the room, she closed the door and said, "Grace, I want you to answer this question honestly." I nodded my head. Marta was looking at the floor. People look at the floor when bad things have happened or are about to happen. Knowing this made me even more nervous. "Have you told anyone that you are hoping Marta gets sick so that you can have her part?" I put my hands up to my mouth. Suddenly I was super glad that I had never mentioned anything about my old wish to anybody, not even Mimi. It was a relief to be truthful and not get into trouble.

Ms. Perry smiled. She patted me on the shoulder and said, "Okay, Grace. You can go, and please don't say anything to anybody." I walked out the door, but then turned around before she could close it again. "I really like my part," I said. "I know," said Ms. Perry. "I can tell."

After about five minutes Marta and Ms. Perry came out of the room. Marta didn't look 100 percent happy, but later that afternoon she smiled at me. It was the first smile I had ever gotten from the fairy queen.

UNUSUAL THING NUMBER TWO

On Friday, Sammy surprised everyone.

WHAT SAMMY IS SUPPOSED TO DO

WHAT SAMMY DID

We all thought it was great, but Ms. Perry said she had to ask the principal if Sammy could really use the slingshot on stage. Sammy said he had been practicing at home. Of course every single boy who saw him do it was super impressed. This whole acting thing was really changing Sammy's life. Now everyone wanted to be his friend.

THE PLAY INVITATION

On Friday we all got play invitations to take home. I couldn't believe how good they were. Grace F. made them; she is a real artist.

THE WEEKEND

This Saturday and Sunday was a lot like last week's Saturday and Sunday, except that it was raining. Mimi and Robert came over, and Robert couldn't wait to show me what he had. It was a real baseball mitt. I don't know anything about baseball, but it seemed like it was not going to be so easy for him to catch stuff with that big glove on his hand. I was pretty much right about that.

WHAT HAD NEVER HAPPENED BEFORE

Mimi and I could not wait for the weekend to be over and for school to start. I wrote it down in my notebook, because I was pretty sure that kind of thing was probably never going to happen again.

MONDAY MORNING

Right away I could tell that everyone was like me: excited to be at school. This was the week of our big play. How could we not be filled with joy? Even Miss Lois seemed happy. I could tell this because she said we were skipping math and could work on our plant maps instead.

MY PLANT MAP

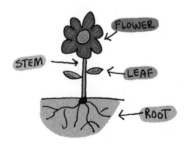

The only annoying thing was that I sit in front of Owen 1, and somehow Ms. Perry had made the big mistake of picking him to be the pooping bear in the play. Now he thought he was the king of every poop joke in the world. All he could talk about were poop jokes. I could tell that even Sammy was getting annoyed, and he loves poop!

WHAT DO YOU CALL A POOPING HIPPO?

MONDAY'S PLAY REHEARSAL

Miss Lois told us that tomorrow was going to be an exciting day. She said, "All the scenery for the play is going to go up, and it's marvelous!" If she was excited about it, I'm sure we would be too.

THE GOOD THING FOR SAMMY

Sammy gets to use the slingshot in the play. Ms. Perry was super happy about this. I think she wanted to give Sammy a reward for working so hard. Even though it was only Monday, he knew almost all of his lines by heart. Marta was happy about that too. She did a lot of smiling.

WHY IT'S SAFE FOR SAMMY TO USE THE SLINGSHOT

THE ONE THING I WAS KNOWING

Our play was going to be a super success!

WHAT HAPPENED ON THE WAY HOME

I know most of Sammy's lines, so I can tell if he is making a mistake, and today he was almost perfect. We did a bit of practicing on the way home, but really he didn't need to. I was the one who needed to practice Marta's part. For some reason her lines were kind of hard to remember. But I was watching her today, and she looked really healthy, so I probably didn't have much to worry about.

WHAT HAPPENED AFTER DINNER

Robert and Mimi came over because Robert wanted to show me his new ball. It's a special ball to use with his new glove. Mimi said Robert is finally letting their dad play catch with him. We played catch a little bit, but I

liked it when we did it without the glove better. After they left I made myself go upstairs
and look over the fairy queen lines one more
time, just to be safe. I had a new secret wish.

MY NEW WISH

TUESDAY

It was really hard to concentrate on math this morning. I was hoping that Miss Lois would let us do fun stuff again, but she didn't. After lunch we worked on our plant projects. Almost everyone has finished a plant map, so what mostly everyone is working on now is the seed stories. We have to pretend to be a seed and write a story about how we got from our parent plant to the ground, where we will grow as a new seedling. Of course the boys are being seeds that are eaten by animals and then pooped out. I was surprised that Miss Lois was okay with this, but I guess it is true nature so she can't do much about it. It was nice to have something creative to work on. It made the afternoon go by faster, which was good because I could hardly wait to get to the auditorium to see the new scenery.

THE FIRST THING I SAID WHEN I SAW THE STAGE

Our whole practice seemed really different from normal. I think having the scenery changed everything. When Marta and I were standing at the side watching the talking trees I said, "I almost feel like a real actress." "Me too!" said Marta. It was amazing!

WHAT I TOLD MOM WHEN I GOT HOME

"I think this play is going to be the best thing I have ever done." Mom came over and gave me a hug. "I can't wait to see it," she said. "I'm really good at my part," I said. "A-bouquet-of-flowers-after-the-show good?" asked Mom. "YES!" I said. "Yes, yes, yes!"

WHAT IS SUPER HARD TO DO

Wait for a day that you know is going to be great. Tomorrow we were going to see our costumes. Even though Mimi said mine wasn't super excellent, I still couldn't wait.

WEDNESDAY

This was a big day for Mimi. Finally she was going to be able to show everyone what she had been working on. When we were halfway to school she said, "I'm so excited, I couldn't eat breakfast." I knew exactly how she felt. "I bet I won't be able to eat breakfast tomorrow," I said.

Miss Lois let us work on our seed stories all morning. I just had the picture part of mine to do, but a lot of people were still doing the writing parts. There were a lot of boys laughing, so I think Miss Lois should have looked more worried than she did.

I picked a maple tree seed for my story, because I like how they spin around like mini helicopters when they fall to the ground, plus they are fun to put on your nose.

LUNCHTIME

At lunchtime Mimi said she was super excited, but she ate her sandwich anyway, because she said she was also super starving. Marta came up to us and said, "I can't wait to see my costume." "I think you're going to like it," said Mimi, and then she gave me a funny look. At first I didn't understand what she was doing, and then I did.

WHAT I WAS KNOWING

Even though Mimi didn't say anything, I knew she was still thinking about me being a little bit sad about not getting the fairy queen part. She was worried about me seeing Marta's costume, but I wasn't going to be jealous. I just knew it. Sometimes you know stuff about yourself, and sometimes you don't. This was a knowing thing!

FINALLY

When we got to the auditorium, Ms. Perry made everyone sit in the audience seats. Usually we stand around on stage. Mimi and Grace F. and some other people were waiting on the stage. "When I call you by name, you can come up and get your costume," said Ms. Perry. I couldn't believe it! For once I was first.

MY COSTUME

LITTLE HAT

REAL GLASSES

THE JACKET

POINTY STICK FOR POINTING

THE BOOK I GET TO CARRY

It was better than Mimi said it would be. My favorite part was the glasses; they had real glass in them. I've always wanted to wear glasses, so getting to wear even just pretend glasses was super fun.

Marta's costume was great. It took a while for her to put it on, but it was worth it—it was really beautiful. It's too bad that she couldn't fly on one of those wire things, because if she was up in the air, she would have for sure looked like a real fairy.

SPARKLY WINGS →

← HEAD THING WITH BEAUTIFUL PAPER LEAVES

SKIRT LOOKS LIKE IT IS MADE OF LEAVES. →

THE SURPRISE GOOD COSTUME AWARD GOES TO...

Sammy's costume!

When Sammy put his costume on, he hardly even looked like Sammy. It was like he was a real king, not a boy pretending to be a king. It was amazing.

THE SECOND SURPRISE GOOD COSTUME AWARD GOES TO...

Owen 1's costume!

He looked so cute. I couldn't believe I was thinking about Owen 1 and *cute* in the same sentence. It was a shock for my brain!

WHAT HAPPENED NEXT

We hardly had time to practice the play. Even though it's only twenty minutes long, we only got through the first half of it. Ms. Perry said not to worry. She was smiling, so I decided to believe her.

WALKING HOME

Everyone stayed late today, so Mimi and Max got to walk home with me and Sammy. Mimi said her favorite costume is Sammy's. "It's mine too!" I said. Sammy just smiled. He seemed kind of quiet. I guess he wasn't used to all the extra attention.

AT NIGHT

Mimi and I made up a new flash code just for tonight. It's thirty-one flashes, which for us is a world record. We did one flash for each letter in I LOVE THE PLAY IT IS GOING TO BE GREAT! That was a lot of flashing. I'm glad we didn't do that every night.

MY TIRED HAND FROM TURNING THE LIGHT ON AND OFF SO MANY TIMES.

PLAY DAY

Today was a double play day. We were having a play, and Miss Lois let us play instead of doing work.

After lunch we went to the auditorium like usual. After the practice Ms. Perry said,

"You are ready!" This was good to hear. I think it made everyone feel less nervous. The only person who still seemed really nervous was Sammy. He was super quiet, which was not normal. Ms. Perry noticed too, because she gave him a special little talk. I saw him laugh, so I guessed she fixed whatever was wrong with him.

WALKING HOME

I walked home with Mimi and Max. We waited for Sammy, but he didn't show up. "Maybe he had to try on his costume one more time, because it's so awesome!" I said. Mimi laughed. "It's good, isn't it?" "It's my favorite one," said Max, and then he looked at me and said, "No offense—yours is good too." "That's okay," I said. "Sammy's is my favorite one too!" "I can't wait for my mom and dad to see it!" said Mimi. "I pretty much made the whole thing all by myself." She was as excited as me, and I was really, really, really excited!

WHAT HAPPENED AT HOME

I told Mom I was too nervous to eat, so she let me have yogurt for dinner. I had to be back at school by six o'clock, even though the show didn't start until seven. Ms. Perry said we needed the extra time just in case. The more I thought about the audience, the more nervous I started to feel. Maybe that was the just-in-case part Ms. Perry was talking about. I was hoping she had some tricks to help us.

WHAT HAPPENED BACK AT SCHOOL

Ms. Perry was all dressed up fancy. She looked great. We were putting on our costumes, but she said, "Put on costumes, everyone!" about ten times anyway. I think she was nervous too.

THE JUST IN CASE

I was helping Marta with her wings when all of a sudden Ms. Perry came rushing into the room. "ATTENTION! ATTENTION!" she shouted. "Gather around, everyone. Quick! Quick!" This was not a good way to calm everyone down. She sounded upset. Two seconds later we all knew why. Sammy was sick!

Throwing-up sick! Throwing-up-with-a-fever sick, and he couldn't be in the play. "IT'S A TOTAL DISASTER!" shouted Owen 1, and he threw his bear hat onto the ground. Now he wasn't looking so cute. I gave him a mean look. "NO, IT'S NOT!" said Ms. Perry. "Pick up your hat, Owen 1! It's unfortunate and sad, but it's not a disaster." Owen 1 put his hat on his head. "Sorry," he said. He was cute again.

CUTE   NOT CUTE   CUTE   NOT CUTE

"These kinds of things happen in the theater all the time, and that's why we prepare for them," said Ms. Perry. She looked around until she found Owen 2. "Owen 2, you're Sammy's understudy, can you do Sammy's part?" Owen 2 looked shocked. He was wearing his knight's uniform, and he held up his shield in front of his body and shook his head. "I don't know it," he said. "Sammy was so good at it, so I thought I didn't have to do it." "That's okay," said Ms. Perry, but I could tell from her face that on her insides she was thinking something different.

THE BAD IDEA TO FIX IT

"Well," said Ms. Perry, "I'll just be the king. We can make it work." She walked over to the costume area and came back wearing

Sammy's crown. "So, everything will go as planned, except that now I'm the king. Do you all understand?" Everyone nodded yes, except for me. "You can't be the king!" I said. "You're too big for the costume!" "Grace," said Ms. Perry. "I know it's not what we planned, but I think everyone will understand who I am if I wear this crown. Plus we can make an announcement to explain the situation."

I shook my head. Ms. Perry was not understanding me! The king costume needed to be in the play! It was the best costume, and the whole reason Mimi was even excited about the play. It was super important! My empathy feelings were working at 100 percent power!

HOW CAN I HELP MIMI?

THE GOOD IDEA TO FIX IT

I felt like I might cry, but then suddenly I had an idea. I shouted it out loud. "Ms. Perry, let me be the king! I fit the costume, and I know all the lines. I really do! I practiced them with Sammy! PLEASE, CAN I DO IT? PLEASE!" It was the perfect and only way to fix everything. I had to do it. Ms. Perry was surprised, and not just a little surprised, but super surprised. "Are you sure?" she asked. "She can do it," said Marta. "I saw her helping Sammy. Plus it's my birthday, and I want Grace to be the king." Now *I* was surprised. Ms. Perry looked at me. I gave her my sad please eyes. Sad please eyes are hard to say no to. Slowly she nodded her head. "YAY!" Marta and I jumped up and down together. "Okay girls, that's enough," said Ms. Perry. She gave me Sammy's crown and pointed to the costume area. "Go get dressed and give me your hat and stick." It was the only part of my outfit that Ms. Perry was going to be able to wear.

While I was getting dressed, Marta came over to see me. "Thank you for doing Sammy's part," she said. "If Ms. Perry was the king I think that would make me super nervous—plus she's too tall." I gave her a smile and then Ms. Perry interrupted us. She had some last-minute instructions for me.

← ME LISTENING TO Ms. PERRY

MS. PERRY'S INSTRUCTIONS

1. If you forget something, look at me and I'll help you.

2. Don't worry too much about where you are standing. What you are saying is more important.
3. When you throw the seed out to the audience, throw it to a grownup in the first row. That way, when I say the wind blew it back, they'll know to throw it back.
4. Don't try to use the slingshot for real. Just pretend to use it. We'll make the bell ring for you.

Then Ms. Perry looked me right in the face and said, "Are you sure about this?" When I nodded she hugged me, just a little, because of course she didn't want to mess up my costume.

WHAT WAS HARD TO BELIEVE

That I was really doing this.

ME BEING NERVOUS

THE SHOW

Right before the show started Ms. Perry went on stage and talked to the audience. She told them how happy she was to be there and how hard we had all worked, and then she said, "Tonight we have a special surprise performance. Unfortunately one of our actors is sick, so tonight the part of the king will be played by Grace Stewart. Thank you, Grace. I will be taking Grace's part of the narrator. And then, at the end of the play we have a special birthday song to sing, so please stay in your seats. Okay, on with the show." After that there was a ton of clapping. It was the kind of clapping that meant every single seat in the whole auditorium had someone in it. That was a lot of people!

WHAT WAS STRANGE

When I heard everyone clapping, I felt 100 percent sick. But the minute I walked out on stage, I was better. I loved being up there. It was kind of like a dream, a super-great day-dream where everything goes exactly how you want it to. And the parts where people laughed after I said something funny—those were the best parts!

THE SEED

The whole play went by super fast. I couldn't believe it was almost over. We were already at the part where I throw the seed out into the audience.

I got ready and said, "I can throw this seed. I don't need animals to help me." I looked in the front row for someone to throw it to. All of a sudden I heard my name. "Grace! Grace! Throw it to me! Throw it to me!" It was Robert, and he was standing in the middle of the auditorium waving his arms. I could see Mimi's mom trying to get him to be quiet and sit down, but he was too excited to listen. Everyone in the audience was looking at him.

I knew Ms. Perry would be mad, but I did it anyway. I threw the seed right to Robert.

ROBERT WITH HIS ARMS IN THE AIR. HE IS READY!

He caught it! Just like I knew he would. Then I heard Ms. Perry say, "But the wind grabbed the seed and threw it back to the king." I looked at Robert and tapped my hands together. Robert pulled his arm back and threw the seed over the whole audience right back to me. It was an excellent throw. The audience went crazy! They clapped and whistled, and clapped some more. It was something I could hardly believe, even though I was standing there and listening with my own two ears.

THE SLINGSHOT

After that it didn't even really matter that I messed up the slingshot part. Sammy would have done it perfectly, but I took too long to get ready and the bell rang before I even pretended to shoot the seed. I don't think anyone cared, though. They clapped anyway, even though I did it wrong.

WHAT IS REALLY FUN TO DO

1. Sing "Happy Birthday" with an auditorium full of people. Marta was happy about that and did a fancy fairy twirl.
2. Bow on stage while standing next to your best friend.

ME AND MIMI ON STAGE TOGETHER

WHAT IS GREAT BUT NOT EASY TO DO

Hold a whole bunch of flowers.

Mom and Dad gave me flowers, Augustine Dupre gave me flowers, and Mimi's mom made Robert give me a flower. There was also lots of hugging. Holding flowers and hugging is not easy either. When Mimi's mom gave me a hug she said, "Grace, you were the star of the stage!" That was better than all the flowers in the world. It was also a huge surprise.

Sometimes surprises like that can make you cry even if you think you won't.

WHAT HAPPENED NEXT

I changed out of my costume and met Mom and Dad and Augustine Dupre in my classroom. It was fun, but not as fun as the play.

WHAT I FORGOT TO DO AT NIGHT

I was so tired that I 100 percent forgot to flash my lights for Mimi. It was okay, though—I knew she'd forgive me.

FRIDAY

Mimi and I talked about the play all the way to school. She said she was sure that Robert was going to love me for the rest of my life. I didn't tell her about being the king just for her. It didn't matter—everything had worked out perfectly, and that was the part that mattered. Except for Sammy—that part was not perfect. Even Mimi was sad for him. It wasn't fair. He had done all that practicing and now he had missed his big chance to be the star on stage.

I BET MISSING THE SHOW MADE SAMMY FEEL EVEN WORSE!

By the time we got to school Mimi and I had a plan, and that plan was to talk to Ms. Perry.

WHAT WAS NOT GOOD

Sammy was still sick, and Ms. Perry was gone. Miss Lois said Ms. Perry would be back in a few weeks for a goodbye lunch, but until then, she wasn't coming back. Then Miss Lois said, "Now please sit down so we can start class." Normally I listen to Miss Lois, but today I didn't—I couldn't help it. Instead of listening to her, I made her listen to me.

IT'S NOT FAIR FOR SAMMY. HE PRACTICED REALLY HARD AND COULD EVEN USE THE REAL SLINGSHOT. WE SHOULD DO THE PLAY AGAIN SO HE CAN DO HIS PART!

USING MY PROJECTING VOICE

After I finished talking I walked to the door. I was sure she was going to send me to see Mr.

Harris, the principal. But Miss Lois surprised me. She said, "Just Grace, where do you think you're going? Please sit in your seat." And then she winked at me. I couldn't believe it. Maybe I was wrong. Maybe she had something in her eye? I looked around, but there was no one to ask. For the whole rest of the morning I watched her to see if she would do it again, but she didn't. I thought she might call me over to have a talk when it was lunchtime, but she didn't do that either.

LUNCHTIME

Mimi said Miss Lois probably had gotten an eyelash in her eye. "Because really, she is not a winking kind of person." Then she said, "You're lucky. I thought for sure you'd get sent to the principal." I agreed. It was all kind of mysterious.

WHAT MIMI WAS RIGHT ABOUT

As soon as we got back from lunch Miss Lois said I had to go to the office to see Mr. Harris. Usually when you get in trouble it happens right away, so you are not so surprised. When it happens much later it is not something you are expecting. When you are not expecting something your face can go super red with embarrassment. It's not a good feeling.

I walked out of class as fast as I could, but I could tell that everyone was watching me. By the time I got to Mr. Harris's office I was really nervous.

WHAT WAS UNEXPECTED

As soon as I walked into Mr. Harris's office he looked up and smiled. "Sit down, Grace," he said. "How are you today?" "Okay," I answered. "Not too tired from the play?" he asked. I shook my head no. "I've been hearing a lot about you today," he said. I held my breath. This was it. This was the getting-in-trouble part—it was about to happen, I could tell. And then Mr. Harris surprised me.

"I've had a talk with Miss Lois and Ms. Perry, and we've decided to do something about your idea. As soon as Sammy is better, we'll have an assembly and show the play to some of the other classes. Once we have that date you can invite your family, and of course we'll invite Sammy's family to sit in. That way they'll be able to see you both in the roles that you practiced for."

I couldn't see my face, but I'm sure it looked just like this.

Mr. Harris waited for me to get back to normal and didn't say anything else. He was very patient. I bet he sees a lot of surprised faces in his office. After a few seconds I said, "Uh, thank you." Mr. Harris stood up and said, "Well, I guess we'd better get you back to class." On the way out Miss W., his secretary, stopped me and said, "Grace, this is for you. I was going to send it down to Miss Lois, but since you're here you can just take it." It was an envelope with a card. I could tell that without even opening it. On my way down the hall I took the card out. On the outside was a drawing of a big smiling star.

This was the inside.

Grace,
Thank you for being a star on and off the stage.
Your Friend,
Ms. Perry

Sometimes a sentence can change a day. I knew that already, but it was nice to have it happen again.

Book
10

WHAT GRACE WILL BE THINKING ABOUT IN HER NEXT BOOK